EMILIO

JM Castilla

EMILIO

Julia Mercedes Castilla

PIÑATA BOOKS
ARTE PÚBLICO PRESS
HOUSTON, TEXAS
1999

This volume is made possible through grants from the National Endowment for the Arts (a federal agency), Andrew W. Mellon Foundation, and the City of Houston through The Cultural Arts Council of Houston, Harris County.

Piñata Books are full of surprises!

Piñata Books
An Imprint of Arte Público Press
University of Houston
Houston, Texas 77204-2174

Cover illustration and design by Giovanni Mora

Castilla, Julia Mercedes.
Emilio / by Julia Mercedes Castilla.
p. cm.
SUMMARY: A young immigrant from Central America finds it difficult to learn English and adjust to life in the big city of Houston, Texas.
ISBN 1-55885-271-9 (pbk. : alk. paper)
[1. Emigration and immigration Fiction. 2. Hispanic Americans Fiction.] I. Title.
PZ7.C2687243 Em 1999
[Fic]—dc21 99-29481
CIP

∞ The paper used in this publication meets the requirements of the American National Standard for Information Sciences—Permanence of Paper for Printed Library Materials, ANSI Z39.48-1984.

9 0 1 2 3 4 5 6 7 8 10 9 8 7 6 5 4 3 2 1

If, dear reader, you have ever felt awkward,
out of place, or different — this book is dedicated to you.
Que el Espíritu Santo te ilumine.
—*JMC*

Another Day of Dread

Emilio missed his hot *caldo,* with tortillas. He salivated, almost tasting the potatoes, the small pieces of bone-meat, the cilantro that made *caldo* taste so good. Every morning he awoke craving the old foods he loved. Why was he having such a difficult time in this strange land while Jaime and Victoria seemed to be getting along well?

Emilio sat by the side of the bed, not quite awake, and yet dreading the day ahead of him. He flopped back and slid under the covers, still warm and welcoming.

"Vamos, Emilio, get going. What's happening to you? Back home you were up before the rooster and now if I don't get you out of bed you lie there like a zombie. *Apúrese muchacho*, hurry, you're going to be late for school," said his mother, pulling the covers off.

Emilio couldn't open his eyes. "I don't feel well, Mama. I better not go to school today," he said, turning his face away. He had gone to bed late and was not in the mood to face another school day.

He didn't understand what was happening to him. He didn't sleep as well as he did back in his hometown of Conchagua. He missed his old house, the sounds of the animals nearby, the fields where he played and worked, and—most of all—he missed his father. He felt different, as if his body belonged to another person. It had been six months since he'd arrived in Houston. His mother, Herminia, and his oldest brother, Jaime, had left home a year before. Emilio and his younger sister, Victoria, had stayed behind with their grandparents while his mother found work in Houston.

"You aren't sick. Get up, go to school." Herminia put her hands on her hips and stared at her son. "We came to this country so you, your brother, and sister could get an education and do better than we did. No excuses; be ready in ten minutes," ordered his mother. Her dark hair seemed to trail behind her as she left the room.

"Sí señora, but I really don't feel good," said Emilio, not moving a muscle. His mind kept going back to the place where he had lived all his life.

Emilio would be twelve in a month—almost a man, according to the tradition in his *pueblo*. His papa had always said that a man should be strong. His eyes filled with tears every time he thought about his father, killed by the guerrillas a couple of years before. If Papa were alive, everything would be different, thought Emilio, rubbing his eyes. For a long time his body refused to move. He didn't want to leave the memories of home, before violence changed his life.

"Hurry, Emilio, breakfast is ready!" shouted her mother, opening the door of the room for the second time.

"I'm coming," said Emilio, pulling on his pants and shirt, his thin body moving around the room in a daze, while he looked for his shoes, socks, and school books.

With his uncombed hair, his shirt hanging over his pants, and the books under his arm, Emilio ran to the kitchen for breakfast.

"Go wash your hands and face, and comb your hair. You look as if you slept with your clothes on, like you did back home. I've told you over and over, you have got to give a good impression in school," said his mother.

Emilio didn't have the energy to argue. It was the same every day. His mama had to tell him to wash as if he were a small child. He just didn't see any reason to do it, when he had never done it before. He didn't understand why his mother now thought washing was important.

"Mama, why can't you fix a real breakfast like you did at home?" asked Emilio.

"*This* is home now, and you know I don't have time for that. I'm already late for work. Eat and don't give me a hard time. Jaime and Victoria already left. You're always dragging behind," said his mother, rushing through the kitchen, opening and closing drawers and cabinets as she organized everything around her. "You always make me late."

Emilio couldn't get used to eating cereal. It wasn't like any food he knew. His mother said cereal was healthy, nutritious, and easy to prepare, but he didn't care for it.

Leaving most of his breakfast untouched, he grabbed a piece of bread and a couple of books and without saying anything he left.

He covered the four blocks from his home to the school, walking as if there were a prize for being last. At school he didn't feel right. Even though several of his classmates spoke Spanish and talked to him sometimes, he was lonely. In his hometown, even Mexico was *el Norte.* He didn't have any friends, as if he were invisible. Emilio wanted to cry but didn't dare. "Men don't cry," his father had said to him often.

Emilio was a few minutes late for science class. The teacher looked at him accusingly and said something in English he didn't understand. He could feel the stares of his classmates as he walked with his head down. He sat in the back of the room.

"You aren't to go to recess. The teacher wants you to stay here to work on your science homework," said José, a boy with dark curly hair, who usually translated what the teacher said to him. His classmate seemed to enjoy being the carrier of bad news.

"Está bien," said Emilio. The idea rather

pleased him. If he was alone no one would bother him. He could read, write on the blackboard, or just daydream.

Emilio had attended school for several months without understanding a word of what the teachers were saying. At the end of the day a bilingual teacher gave him a review—in Spanish—of the subjects taught during the day. He enjoyed this part of school.

"Don't worry, Emilio, soon you'll understand English and you'll have lots of friends," said the bilingual teacher when he felt discouraged. She was a nice lady with penetrating eyes that made him nervous.

It didn't seem possible to him that one day he could master the language that seemed to tangle his tongue. Emilio liked to learn, but he thought he would never learn English.

"Are you dumb?" shouted a boy as he went by Emilio at the cafeteria during lunch hour.

Emilio didn't understand most of what the bully said, but he guessed it was an insult. Since his arrival at the school, the bigger boy had made Emilio's life more difficult than it already was. Matt and his friend Cato had made it their business to torment him.

The smell of food in the cafeteria made Emilio sick. He couldn't understand why the food smelled so different. It made him nauseous, and he could hardly eat.

"Matt asked you if you were dumb." A girl Emilio had not seen before spoke to him in Spanish. She sat at the same table where he had been sitting by himself.

"I'm not dumb. He's the dumb . . ." Emilio felt the blood rush to his face. He stood, ready to face the boy who had insulted him.

The girl put her hand on Emilio's shoulder. "Sit down. It's better to ignore him." Her soft voice calmed him.

"How do you know my name?" Emilio tried to get hold of himself.

"My name is Clara. We take a class together. The teacher calls your name. You never look around, or you would have seen me. I've been here for a year. I'm from Mexico. Where are you from?"

Clara and Emilio talked about their countries, their families, and their new life. They were the same age. Clara was thin and petite like him. She had shiny, long, black hair and he thought she had the sweetest smile he had ever seen. Emilio felt content, a feeling he had not had for a long time.

"You're having a bad time here, aren't you? It was the same with me," said Clara. "I didn't think I'd ever get used to being here, but believe me, you will. Now that I understand and speak English, I have lots of friends I'll be glad to introduce to you. Would you like to go to a baseball game with me and my friends after school?"

Emilio didn't answer right away. The question took him by surprise. He felt excitement, and yet he was afraid. He didn't like the way his classmates and other people looked at him and didn't think Clara's friends would look at him any differently. Almost without his consent he shrugged and said, "Okay, maybe . . ." He was secretly thrilled.

"I'll meet you at three-thirty at the school's main entrance," said Clara, getting up from the table.

Emilio stayed behind for a few minutes. Panic struck him. Clara's friends were strangers. What could he say to them? They would make fun of him. He might as well go home and listen to the radio in his room . . .

"Coward!" yelled the bully in English, pushing Emilio out of his chair.

Emilio got up and pushed him back. "Don't talk to me like that. I don't understand what you said but I won't let you push me around and insult me any more," yelled Emilio in Spanish. His father wouldn't have liked Emilio's feeling sorry for himself. He could almost see his papa in front of him, telling him to be his own person. Emilio wouldn't let his father down.

The bully didn't seem to expect a reaction from Emilio. He had been mean to him for months without any retaliation. Surprised, Matt stood with his mouth open.

"Péguele, hit him!" someone yelled to Emilio.

"No, I don't want to go around hitting people. But no one is going to put me down again," said Emilio, walking away.

"I can't believe you stood up for yourself. It's about time. I'm proud of you," said Clara who had stopped at a nearby table to talk to a couple of friends.

"Gracias," he mumbled and continued walking toward the exit. He didn't want to give the bully another chance once he got over his shock.

"I'll see you later," Emilio heard Clara yelling. He waved his hand.

Emilio decided not to think about Matt and the other kids who seemed to enjoy insulting him, at least not today. He would not let them spoil the moment. For the first time in months he had a friend, his first and only friend in this country.

New Friends

Emilio was hiding behind the wall of the school's main building when he saw Clara coming down the steps, in front of the main entrance, where they had agreed to meet. He had been debating with himself about going to the baseball game. His brother Jaime kept on telling him he should go out and make friends, instead of brooding all day. His brother might be right, thought Emilio. He had to try.

Gathering his courage, Emilio came out of hiding. Immediately he regretted it, but it was too late; Clara had already seen him.

"Emilio, I thought you weren't coming. I was getting ready to leave. I'm glad you decided to join me. Let's go, I know we'll have a great time. You'll see," said Clara, walking toward him with that sweet smile.

"I don't know if I should. Your friends may not like me. I think I'd I better go home. Maybe another time, when I can speak English and feel like they might accept me. I'd like to be your friend though."

"I'm your friend, but you'll never learn if you stay away from people," said Clara, grabbing Emilio by the arm. "You have to start to *really* live here in this country, or you'll never belong.

That's what my mother and my teachers used to tell me. Come on, let's go."

"Where is the game?" asked Emilio, trying to hide his fear. He would have given anything to be in the safety of his room.

"It's at the high school, just a few blocks away. Marcia and Pablo wanted me to walk with them, but I told them I was going with a new friend and would meet them there. I wanted to have time to tell you about them."

"Okay." The idea pleased Emilio. It would make it easier for him to know who these kids were.

They walked quietly for half a block before Clara said anything. She seemed to be looking for the right words to describe her friends.

"They're really nice *muchachos*, nothing like Matt and his *amigos*. Marcia and Pablo are twins and are very smart. They were born down in San Antonio and moved to Houston two years ago. They understand Spanish but don't speak it well." Clara paused for a minute to look in both directions before they crossed the street.

"How did you meet them?" asked Emilio, wondering why he had never seen them.

"We live in the same neighborhood and go to the same bus stop. You'll like my friends. Besides Pablo and Marcia there is Katy, who lives by my house. She's the only one who doesn't go to our school. She goes to a parochial school. My mother says her parents don't like public schools because they think the students don't get a good education and have no discipline. They also want her to learn about God. She's an only child. It must be nice to be the only one. I'd like that." Clara seemed to wait for Emilio's reaction, but he didn't say anything.

"There is also Ali, a shy boy, kind of like you. He's from somewhere in Jordan, I think. Ali isn't his real name but we can't pronounce his name. Marcia met him at school and he's been hanging around with us for a couple of months."

"They sound all right. Do you think they will like me?" Emilio didn't expect them to be nice to him.

"I know they will. Here we are. Hurry, I see Pablo over there," said Clara, waving her hand to someone in the crowd, as they entered the high school stadium.

Emilio had never been to a stadium. Back home kids played soccer—the only sport he knew—anywhere they could kick a ball. It's *big*, he thought, looking at the bleachers around the field. Emilio lost his confidence again. There were so many older kids. He felt as if all of them were coming at him with dislike on their faces.

"I don't think I can do this, Clara. I'd better go home." Emilio felt sick to his stomach. He couldn't understand why he felt so scared. He almost felt that he might burst into tears. Why was he so afraid, after all the experiences, so much worse, he had been through in his own homeland?

"No way, you're not going to leave now." Clara pulled him by the arm.

"Hi, Clara, we've been waiting for you. The others are saving our seats," said a short, stocky boy about Emilio's age.

"Pablo, this is my friend Emilio."

"Hi, Emilio," said Pablo in better Spanish than Emilio expected. "Clara told us about you. She said you recently came to this country. I'm glad you're here. Come on, follow me. It isn't easy to try to save places with this crowd. These kids don't respect seat-keeping." Pablo burst out laughing, his dark, round eyes bright with excitement.

"Hi," whispered Emilio, following the other two. He liked Pablo. With Clara and Pablo on his side he might make it through the game.

The shouts drowned the introductions, giving Emilio time to adjust to his surroundings. The game began. He had no idea who was playing, so Emilio's interest was not on the game, but rather on his new friends. Sitting at the end of the row, by Clara, he felt free to study the group.

Marcia, Pablo's twin, unlike her brother, was slender and had a studious look, Emilio thought. She wore glasses and her brown hair was neatly pulled back in a ponytail. She seemed curious about Emilio and glanced at him often. A girl with red hair sat by Clara.

"I'm glad you could come," said Katy in Spanish, sticking her head behind Clara.

"Gracias," said Emilio, turning as red as Katy's hair. He couldn't think of anything else to say. Even if he could speak English, he didn't think he would be able to utter a word. It surprised him that she spoke to him in Spanish.

"Would you like a piece of gum?" She asked, extending her hand to him.

"Gracias," he said again, feeling like an idiot. He took a piece of gum from the package and smiled at her.

"I know Spanish. I do have an accent, but I hope you can understand me," said Katy, going back to watching the game.

"Yes," he mumbled. Emilio understood her perfectly but he was puzzled. Why were this particular group of kids being so nice to him? Did they feel sorry for him? He wouldn't like that. He didn't need charity from anyone.

Yes, that must be it. Clara's friends felt sorry for him. He was sure she had told them to be nice to him and to treat him as if he were a poor defenseless child whom no one liked.

The boy they called Ali turned his tawny face toward Emilio and smiled, making him even angrier. He had the largest, darkest eyes Emilio had ever seen. Ali said something Emilio didn't understand. He didn't want to talk to him anyway and turned his face the other way. Why were they all smiling at him as if it were a task?

Emilio's head was ready to explode, he was so upset. If he could just go back to his country where he belonged . . . He would not take charity any longer. As soon as Ali turned his face away, Emilio rushed out.

He didn't look back. The only thought in his mind was to go home and hide forever. He would take a bus back to his own country. He would somehow find the money for the fare. He knew he would be all right once he was in his hometown. His grandparents would be glad to see him.

His mind was a million miles away, engrossed in plans to go back to his native land. He though he heard steps behind him, but didn't look back. The roar from the stadium seemed to follow him as he walked on the lonely street.

Emilio didn't have time to react. He saw a hand in front of his eyes. Everything went blank. When he came to he found himself on the ground, his nose bleeding.

Everything happened so fast that it took Emilio a moment to fully realize what had happened. He moaned in pain.

"This is where I wanted to see you. You'll never make me look like an idiot in front of my friends again," yelled Matt, kicking Emilio as hard as he could.

"Yeah," said someone else, kicking Emilio even harder. "This ought to teach you. Now, let's go."

Cruel laughter resounded in Emilio's brain. Matt and Cato laughed mercilessly as they disappeared behind the school's gate. "Now we are even, dumb kid."

Emilio wanted to make the boys pay so badly, he almost threw himself on the two bullies with his bare hands. But they were at least half a head taller than he, and a lot stronger. Cato was quite a mixture. Every existing race and nationality seemed to be present in this human being who took pride in being mean. Emilio had gone to extremes to stay out of his way in school.

If only he had seen them coming he wouldn't have let them hit him. Emilio was a fast runner. Back in his own country, he'd had to outrun foxes when they went after his family's chickens, and mean stray dogs who'd chased him . . . and some men who had meant to do him harm, too. He could also squeeze his body through narrow openings and out of slippery hands. But these two sneaky kids had hit him from behind.

Emilio knew what the word *dumb* meant. He had heard it often enough from some of his classmates who thought that because he didn't speak English he was dumb. He would show them.

"You aren't worth anything. I spit on your faces," said Emilio, spitting as far as he could.

Emilio stood up, cleaned his bloody nose with the sleeve of his shirt, and walked away. He swore to make the cruel boys eat their insults, even if he had to postpone fleeing the country. His father would have wanted him to defend his good name, and he would do just that.

Why Me?

With a heavy heart and a sore body Emilio walked home, asking himself over and over, *Why me?* What was wrong with him? Why was he the target of either hate or charity? Why couldn't he be like the other boys? Why did he feel so foreign and different?

"Did you get into a fight?" asked Jaime as Emilio walked into the small kitchen. His brother was fixing a sandwich.

"I don't want to talk about it," said Emilio, walking away.

"Where are you going? Come here, tell me about the fight," insisted Jaime, grabbing his younger brother by the shoulder.

"Leave me alone. I don't have to do what you want." Emilio tried to get away. "Let go of me."

"What's the matter with you? Why are you so mad? Go, I don't care. It's your business if you want to let people walk all over you, then come home with a bloody nose and hide like a scared cat." Jaime let go of Emilio and went back to his sandwich.

Even his own brother was against him, thought Emilio, fighting the tears that filled his eyes. Emilio wished he could be more like Jaime, who looked like their father—tall, and good-looking. His brother had the same big brown eyes with long eyelashes his papa had. It pained him to see his father in Jaime's face but not in his own. According to his mother, Emilio was the image of her own baby brother who had died as a child–small, frail-looking, and shy.

Not able to contain his tears any longer, Emilio rushed to the room the brothers shared. He closed the door. Jaime, who was outgoing and sociable, didn't seem to think that a bedroom had any other use than for sleeping, so Emilio could be alone to do all the brooding he needed.

"Why do you like to be by yourself? You don't play with me like you used to," said Victoria, coming into the room. "It's boring to come home after school. I don't like apartments. There is no place to run and play like we did in the fields."

Emilio looked at his younger sister with annoyance. He didn't feel like talking, or playing, but Victoria had a special place in his life. She was still a child, a beautiful girl everyone loved.

"I don't want to play, Victoria. I'm not a child now. I want to be alone."

"You liked playing when we were home. Everything is different here. I wish we were back in our old house. We had so much fun. I don't have any fun here. You're not the same, no one is the same. Mama is never home. Jaime thinks he's so cool and is always going somewhere, and you don't want to do anything or talk or nothing."

Victoria's pretty face looked sad.

"Are you also sad? I didn't know," said Emilio, surprised. "I though it was only me. You never said anything. I also wished we were back. I don't know why we had to come to this country. It's pretty but it's so different. We don't even speak the same language. I hate school." Emilio couldn't bring himself to say more to his sister.

"Would you play a game with me? I already finished my homework." Victoria pushed her long, brown hair back, took off the hair pin that had slipped down, and secured it again.

"If you leave me alone I'll play with you later, " said Emilio to pacify the girl.

"Okay." Victoria walked out of the room.

A few minutes later she came back. Victoria looked at her brother for a few moments. Emilio was on his bed, staring at the ceiling. He pretended not to see her.

"I'm glad I don't have to study in English yet. I will next year, though. Will you help me with my homework then?" Victoria was eight years old and still went to bilingual classes.

Emilio gave up. His sister would do anything to get his attention. "You already know more than I do. You'll be helping me instead. I don't think I'll ever learn this language. I'm not good at it." He was silent for a moment. "When we were home we didn't even know we were poor. Everyone in Conchagua was like us, while here we are poor and different, and I don't like the way people look at us."

"How do they look at us?" asked Victoria.

"Are the kids in your school nice to you? Don't they make fun of you and call you dumb because you don't speak this crazy language?" Emilio thought his sister had not understood his question.

"No, not really. All of them speak Spanish. There are two kids I don't like. They're plain bad. *Señorita* Jimenez says they are unruly children. Fred hits everybody and is always fighting, and Luciano is . . ." Victoria went on and on about the troublemakers in her class.

Emilio stopped listening to his sister's stories. His troubled mind kept on saying, *Why me?* Why did everyone pick on him? Even his mother seemed to blame him for not doing this, or for doing that. Jaime and Victoria could do no wrong.

"You promised to play a game with me. Do you want to play bingo?" asked Victoria as she finished talking about Fred and Luciano, who seemed to provide a lot of excitement for Victoria and her classmates.

"I don't like to play bingo. It's a stupid game," said Emilio crossly.

"But you promised." Victoria looked as if she were going to cry.

"Está bien, but only one game. I'm not in the mood to play silly games." Emilio could never say

no to his sister and she seemed to know how to make him do what she wanted.

Emilio and Victoria were very close, and he felt the need to protect her. Back in Conchagua, he used to take her everywhere he went, and she loved it. Now he was miserable most of the time, and never went anywhere. Victoria rushed to bring the game from the room she shared with her mother. She hurried back, carrying a red cardboard box. She took out the worn-out cards and gave one to her brother.

"Let's call Jaime. It'll be more fun with him. I'll go get him." Victoria rushed out of the room again.

"He won't play with us," said Emilio, but Victoria was already gone.

The girl came back pouting. "He said he's too old to play games with us. I don't want people to grow up."

Who did his brother think he was? Since Emilio and Victoria came to Houston, Jaime had looked at them as if they were stupid children he didn't need to bother with.

"We'll see about that," said Emilio, leaving the room in a hurry.

Victoria followed him.

"Jaime, do you think you're better than us? I can play with Victoria but you can't? I'm tired of your attitude. You're only two years older than me, so what is your problem?" Emilio stumbled on his words, he was so mad. It felt good to release the tension and let go of some of the anger he had inside him.

"What are you talking about?" asked Jaime, his mouth half-filled with food.

"Don't play dumb with me. You think you're too good, too smart and too, too . . . whatever, to play with Victoria or even talk to me. Being tall or good-looking doesn't mean you're better. If Papa were here, he wouldn't let you behave like this."

"You were the one that didn't want to talk to me. I asked you to tell me why you had a bloody nose, and you didn't want to talk about it," said Jaime. "Anyway, I don't like children's games. Teenagers do different things than kids. You and Victoria are just children. Why are you so mad anyway? What's gotten into you?" Jaime looked puzzled by Emilio's outburst.

"*¿Qué pasa, muchachos?* Why are you yelling? You didn't even hear me come in," said Herminia, rushing into the kitchen. She put her large brown purse on the kitchen table and deposited a grocery bag on the narrow counter by the stove.

"I don't know what's wrong with Emilio, Mama. [illegible] and insulting me since h[illegible] fight in school or somew[illegible]nt with me."

"Jai[illegible] play with Victoria and m[illegible] tell us what to do.

He thinks he's so cool because he can speak English and knows people and all. He used to be different," said Emilio.

"Jaime is mean. He won't play with us," said Victoria, running to her mother.

Herminia did not seem to see Victoria. "Fighting and going at each other's throats isn't going to help us get anywhere. Everything is different here, so all of you get used to it. Jaime, you're to look out for your brother and sister. We talked about that before they came to join us. Emilio, you have to stop living in the past. We can't go back. We have to go forward, even if it's difficult. I've worked very hard to get you all here."

"But, Mama—" said Emilio.

"No *buts*. I also miss home. I know it isn't easy to come to a foreign country. Jaime and I stayed with your uncle Pedro and his family for months before I could get a job so I could send for you and Victoria. I wasn't prepared for anything but farm labor. I was lucky to have found a decent position, helping with the produce at the grocery store. There wasn't much I could without the language and proper training. I don't want this to happen to you."

Herminia's words left her children speechless. In the past their mother had limited herself to taking care of their needs and telling them what to do. Emilio didn't know how his mother could come up with so much stuff. Was she also changing? Where was the family he knew?

"I hope you all have done your homework. Jaime, put those groceries away. Emilio, wash your hands, get me an onion, and take the trash out. Victoria, set the table while I go change my clothes."

Emilio ran his hands through the faucet, grabbed the plastic grocery bag with the day's garbage, and rushed out of the apartment. He needed fresh air to collect his thoughts.

A Bad Day

How was he going to face Clara after running away from the stadium without even saying good-bye? She didn't mean any harm by asking her friends to pretend to be nice to him. Still, she shouldn't have done it. Emilio kept on trying to defend his actions. He walked to the school corner and then backtracked towards home for the third time. He was already ten minutes late for class.

"What are you up to, kid?" asked a policeman, sticking his head from a blue police car Emilio had not even heard approaching. "Why don't you go to school?"

"¿Qué?" asked Emilio in terror. He feared his legs would give in. He had heard horror stories from classmates and neighbors about the police.

"What are you doing?" asked the officer in a commanding voice.

"Me no English, *señor*," mumbled Emilio.

"Don't pull that one on me. I've been watching you circle around here. Do you think I'm an idiot? *¿Va a esta escuela?"* asked the officer in broken Spanish.

"Sí señor," answered Emilio in a low voice.

"Okay, *vamos*, let's go talk to the principal,"

said the policeman. "Get in the car."

"I can walk there. It's only a block away." It was Emilio's worst moment since he had arrived in the city six months before.

"Get in the car!" shouted the man.

The pavement seemed to move under Emilio's feet. His head spun around, and his legs trembled so hard he didn't think he could walk the few steps to the passenger's door of the vehicle.

"Hurry up! I don't have all day."

Emilio managed to get himself inside. He didn't say a word. Neither did the policeman, who drove to the parking area inside the school grounds.

"Come with me." The officer got out of the car and waited for Emilio to do the same.

As the frightened boy tried to open the door he tripped and fell down. He managed to get up and pick up the books he had been carrying. Emilio felt as small as an ant when he saw the huge officer in front of him. He walked alongside the big man in uniform. "Oh God!" he whispered. Why was he in so much trouble when he hadn't done anything wrong?

Emilio was sure he would wet his pants. The thought filled him with shame. As they entered the school building, the boy felt a warm trickle running down his leg. He froze.

"Sir, I need to go to the bathroom."

"That's an old trick. *Vamos*," said the policeman.

"Por favor," implored Emilio, sobbing, as he looked down at his wet pants.

"I guess it's too late," said the officer. "I'll be— Why are you so afraid? Are you hiding something?"

"No, I promise. I haven't done anything wrong. I just didn't want to come to school today because I had a fight yesterday. Please let me go, *señor policía.* I promised I won't do it again." Emilio didn't know what he was promising, since he was not quite sure what he had done. He would have agreed to anything.

"Were you going to come inside the building or were you planning to get into some kind of trouble?" asked the policeman, looking sorry for Emilio.

"What?" asked Emilio, not quite understanding the man's Spanish, and overwhelmed by what was happening to him.

The officer repeated the question.

"Yes, I was going." Emilio saw the wet spot growing down his blue jeans. Even his left sock felt wet now.

"If I ever see you again roaming the streets when you should be in school, I'll take you to the principal, and if necessary to the police station. Go on now. You're not going to have a good day with those wet pants. *Adios."*

The officer left Emilio in the middle of the

main hallway. He didn't know what to do. His first impulse was to go back home before anyone saw him. On second thought he decided against it. He couldn't risk meeting the policeman again. The next best thing was to go to the bathroom, clean himself, and then find a place to hide for the rest of the day.

There was no one in sight. In ten minutes or so kids would be running all over as they prepared to change classes. Emilio wasn't going to wait for that. He walked as quietly as he could until he reached the bathroom.

Luck was not around for Emilio on that day. He opened the door slowly and went in. At that moment someone came out from one of the stalls.

"You wet your pants! You wet your pants!" yelled José, the boy who translated punishments and assignments for him. "Wait till I tell the others. This is *gooood.*"

"I didn't. It's water. Don't—" Emilio let his body fall to the floor.

José had rushed out laughing.

If he stayed there he would be the joke of the day, ridiculed and mocked by everyone in the school, he thought. And he could not risk going home. He would never be able to show his face again. Emilio looked for a place to hide.

José and his friends would be back any minute. First period would be over just about then. He had to find a place to conceal himself.

The window by the sink caught his attention. Emilio was glad he was at ground level.

He tried to lift up the heavy glass panel but it seemed to be stuck. He struggled for several minutes without moving it one inch. A roar outside the door reached him. He had to get out of there, but the window didn't budge.

"Please, open," he said aloud.

Emilio looked up in despair and saw two small loops on top of the window frame. His fingers, numb from pushing, managed to unlock the window. He heard feet approaching. As fast as he could, he lifted the window frame and squeezed his body out of the bathroom.

"So you wet your pants. Come, Emilio, we want to see you. You're not running all over the school with wet pants, ha, ha," said voices behind him.

He heard laughter as he slid through the window before the owners of the voices could spot him. Emilio ran to the end of the building looking for a bush, or anything that would protect him. A bed of azaleas bordered the building. He squeezed his body between the wall and the bushes, grateful he was small and thin. The azaleas were in full bloom, and they reminded him of the colorful flowers back in Conchagua.

His wet pants made him feel cold. Emilio was glad it wasn't raining. There was not a lot of room for him to move. He sat against the wall with his knees up and his feet under the plants.

Time went by so slowly, Emilio thought the day would never end. It seemed to him that he had been looking at azaleas for so long his eyes would never again see anything but purple. His legs were numb. He was going to stretch and stand for a moment when he heard noises.

If anybody saw him he would just die of embarrassment. Emilio looked at his pants. They were almost dry. Still, he couldn't get out. How would he explain his being there? Besides, José would make sure the whole school knew about his wet pants. There wasn't anything else to do but wait.

"Do you have a cigarette?" asked a hoarse voice so close to Emilio he thought someone was addressing him.

"Yes, I have two," answered his companion. "I was going to get more but my father came into the room before I could grab them all. I was hoping for at least four or five."

Emilio positioned himself so he could see through the branches. He didn't know the boys. They probably were in the eighth grade.

"What are you waiting for, give one to me," said the boy with the hoarse voice, turning around to face the bushes.

For a moment Emilio was sure the two boys would discover him. The boy with the hoarse voice sounded mean. He didn't need another Matt on his case. Emilio didn't dare breathe.

"Well? Are you coming with me to smoke behind the trash cans? Or you just want to stay here till someone catches us?" asked the mean boy.

"Sure, sure," answered the other voice meekly, as they walked away.

Smoking wasn't something Emilio had thought much about. His mother said it wasn't good for you, but the men back home smoked all the time. About three months ago his mama had chewed out Jaime when she found him smoking. Emilio was curious. It was a grown-up thing to do. Maybe one day he'd try one.

"Where do you think he went? I bet Mr. Smith got hold of him and punished him. I wished you had seen him. His pants were wet all the way down to his shoes. He was a mess."

Emilio recognized José's voice. Who was he with? He couldn't see their faces, only the feet of several people standing to the left of where he was.

"I can't believe I missed all the fun. It would have been a perfect revenge for trying to spit on Matt and me. That stupid kid thinks he can stand up to us. I should have hit him harder yesterday," said Cato.

The thought of Cato and Matt tormenting him in front of the whole school because of his wet pants sent a cold chill down Emilio's back. He prayed they wouldn't find him. He caught his breath as he heard Clara's voice.

"Why don't you leave Emilio alone? What has he done to you? It's not fair to pick on him just for the fun of it. He's not as big and strong as you."

"What is it to you? Don't interfere with my business, silly girl. Mind your own," said Cato.

"I don't want to have anything to do with you." Clara's voice sounded weak but firm.

"Daring, aren't you? Go on to your friends and leave me alone. I don't want to fight with a stupid girl."

Emilio wished he could jump over the bushes and hit Cato. How dared he talked to Clara like that. He would find a way to get even.

"Just leave him alone. I mean it," said Clara, walking away as the bell rang. Emilio could see her brown loafers moving alongside the bushes.

In a few minutes the voices and noise faded away. Emilio was again alone waiting for the day to be over. He felt bad for leaving Clara and her friends the day before, but he didn't like her feeling sorry for him either.

After an eternity, Emilio's day behind the bushes was finally over. He waited almost an hour after dismissal before he ventured out of his hiding place. Every bone in his body hurt, along with whatever was inside him that made him so miserable. Could things get any worse?

You Have to Give Me an Excuse!

"How was school?" asked Jaime as Emilio walked into the kitchen.

Emilio had hoped to sneak into his room undetected. He had to change his smelly pants. Since when did Jaime ask him about school? Was he still curious about his bloody nose from the day before? Did he know about the policeman? Had the school called?

"Why?" asked Emilio.

"There is no winning with you; it's bad if I talk to you, and bad if I don't. So what's it going to be? You and Victoria got Mama upset because I didn't pay attention to you, so I'm nice to you and look what I get." Jaime seemed to be in a playful mood.

"Okay." Emilio didn't know what else to say. He didn't feel like talking to anybody, at least not yet. But he would have to tell his mother something. He needed an excuse for not showing up. It had been such a bad day, he wanted it to be over soon.

"*Okay?* That's all you have to say?" Jaime put a spoonful of beans on a tortilla.

"Where did you get those beans?" Emilio was

starving. He hadn't eaten anything since breakfast.

"They were on the stove. I'm just eating a bit. They're cold. Do you want some?" asked Jaime politely.

"Yes, I'm sooo hungry," said Emilio grabbing a plate from the dish rack. He took a tortilla, dumped a big spoonful of beans on top, and ate it with gusto. "Mama must have really talked to you. You're so nice I don't think you're the same person."

"Well, I don't want you telling Mama stories about me." Jaime gave him an accusing look. "You and Victoria have to make friends and leave me alone. I already do enough, having to stay here, taking care of both of you until Mama gets home."

"Whatever. I'm going to do my homework. Where is Victoria?" Emilio stood as far from Jaime as he could. He didn't want his brother to detect the smell of his pants.

"She's at her friend Minerva's. I'll go get her later," said Jaime, taking a soda out from the small refrigerator. He walked to the main room—a combination of den, living and dining room—and turned on the television set. He was through talking to his younger brother.

Emilio changed clothes and hid in his room until his mother called him, that evening. She needed help in the kitchen. His head hurt from worrying. One minute he was ready to get on a bus and go home, and the next he was planning a way to get back at Matt, Cato, José and everyone else who made his life miserable.

Jaime had rushed out of the house as soon as he finished eating. When he was home he was either eating or watching television. Jaime seemed to have something to do every evening. Victoria had managed to talk her mother into letting her spend the night with her friend, and they could walk together to school the next morning. So Emilio was left alone at the table with his mother.

"Why are you so quiet?" asked Herminia.

"I don't have anything to say," responded Emilio, fidgeting with a plastic salt shaker.

"I don't think so. You look strange. Did something happen in school? I'll find out sooner or later so you better tell me now. You have a guilty face," said Herminia, looking worried.

Emilio thought it spooky: His mother seemed almost always to know what was happening to him. The boy didn't answer right away. He didn't know what to say.

"Is it that bad?" asked Herminia.

"I don't know." Emilio got up from the kitchen table and walked to the sink where he deposited his dish, something he automatically did every night.

"Leave that for later. Come, tell me what happened."

"I was only walking. I wasn't doing anything wrong, when this policeman . . ." Emilio's tongue didn't seem to work.

"Out with it, I'm losing my patience," said Herminia.

"It wasn't fair, Mama. I was just a little late when a policeman stopped me. He said I wasn't supposed to be in the street during school hours. He was going to take me to the principal . . . I was so scared, Mama. I didn't mean to wet my pants. He let me go but I couldn't go to class with wet pants. I would have been so embarrassed. I hid all day behind the bushes. You've got to give me an excuse, Mama, please." Emilio knew he wasn't making any sense.

"I didn't get half of what you said. What was that about you wetting your pants? Do you expect me to believe such a story? What did you say about a policeman? Okay, let's start again. You better not lie to me."

"I'm telling you the truth. Please, Mama, believe me," said Emilio getting very upset.

"Okay. If you didn't go to school, what did you do? Don't tell me you wet your pants and hid behind some bushes all day." Herminia seemed annoyed. "I have a lot to do yet, and look at the time. Speak."

"What is the use if you think I'm lying? But if

you don't give me an excuse they'll probably suspend me from school, which is all right with me. I don't like school anyway."

"Emilio, you're making my life more difficult than it already is. Why don't you behave? What's wrong with you? You complain about everything, and you don't like anybody. What am I to do with you?"

"I try, but . . . everything here is so different. The kids in school make fun of me. No one likes me. I'll never learn how to speak English. I wish we were in our *real* home," said Emilio, hoping a miracle would transport them back where they belonged.

Herminia gestured, dismissing his complaints. *"Está bien,* let's try again. Tell me what happened."

Emilio went over the day, from the moment he left home until he came back. Whether his mother believed his story didn't seem important anymore. He had to tell it to someone.

Herminia was silent for such a long time Emilio thought she was mad at him. "Why don't you say something, Mama? You still don't believe me, right?"

"Well, it's such a wild story. First, tell me, why didn't you enter the school? Why were you walking the streets almost half an hour after school started?"

This time it was Emilio who kept quiet. He

didn't want to talk about Clara with his mother. She would never understand.

"Yesterday I had a fight with a boy in school, and I didn't want to face him and have another fight." Emilio thought that was the best he could do to explain.

Herminia looked at him in an strange way. "No one would ever believe you."

"If you don't give me an excuse, I'm dead. Please, Mama, I will never do this again. I promise to get up earlier and go to school on time," said Emilio in a last, desperate plea.

"Your father would have known what to do. It's very difficult for me to be mother and father, especially to boys like you and Jaime." Herminia continued to ponder, making Emilio very nervous.

"Are you going to give me an excuse or not? I bet you would do it for Jaime or Victoria, but for me you won't."

"Emilio! Enough of that! I'm tired of your feeling sorry for yourself. Don't play victim. If you play victim, you'll always be one. Believe me, I know," said Herminia.

The word *victim* seemed to stick in Emilio's brain. His mother didn't cease to surprise him. When did she become so savvy? Just a year ago she didn't say things like that.

Don't play victim, don't play victim. The sentence kept on running inside his mind.

"What is it going to be, Mama? If you don't write an excuse I have to go back home. There is no way I can stay in this city. I'm not afraid to go home by myself. I'll take a bus, or many buses, until I get there. I'll live with *los abuelos.* I'll even walk part of the way if I have to."

Herminia got up from the table. "I didn't go through so much for you to go back. The guerrillas will make you work for them or they'll kill you. You better stop thinking about going back. I can't solve all your problems, Emilio. You have to try to learn the language, study, and stay out of trouble. Now, let me think about this for a while. Go wash the dishes and take the trash out. I'll let you know about this later."

While he washed the dishes he heard his mother quietly leave the apartment. He found it odd since she always let them know where she was going.

Emilio sat down to watch television while he waited for her to return. Every night he watched two or three programs in English, even though he found it difficult to concentrate.

Tonight, even though he didn't understand the dialogue, he suddenly thought he could distinguish words, and he *almost* knew what the characters were saying.

"Where did you go, Mama?" asked Emilio as his mother walked into the room.

"I needed some help with this letter. I went next door, to Dolores' apartment. I'm not—well . . . *This* is why it's so important that you go to school and learn, so you don't have to ask for help." She waved a piece of paper at him. "Having to go to a neighbor to help me write a letter for my son's school because I can't is embarrassing. I don't want you to go through this." Herminia's eyes were moist and her voice trembled.

Emilio didn't like to admit that his mother was almost illiterate. She had told them she had only two years of school and could barely write short sentences. Jaime, Emilio, and Victoria had gone to school since they were six; their mother made sure of it. Emilio remembered his Papa complaining about their absence because he needed their help at home.

His Papa used to say, "I didn't go to any school and I'm doing just fine. Those kids don't need to go to town to learn numbers and letters while I need them here." But Herminia sent them anyway. She said it was only for half a day, so they had the afternoon to work in their small piece of land.

"Did you write the excuse?" asked Emilio anxiously.

"Yes. I'm not writing that you were sick, or had a major catastrophe. I'm not lying to get you out of trouble."

Why didn't she just give it to him? Mothers

were always giving sermons, even when there was no reason. "But it *wasn't* my fault. I didn't do nothing wrong."

"Okay, here," said Herminia. "It's in Spanish, so you have to give it to your bilingual teacher. Dolores doesn't write well in English."

The boy didn't pay much attention to Herminia's explanation. He grabbed the paper and read it.

Dear Teacher:

My son, Emilio Orduz, had a problem on his way to school and could not go to class. Please excuse him for missing school.

Sincerely,
Herminia Orduz

"But Mama, it doesn't say why. This isn't an excuse. The teacher will never believe you wrote it. She'll think I did it."

"It's the truth, isn't it? If they ask me I'll tell them I wrote it. Now go to bed." Herminia seemed exhausted.

"Good night," said Emilio, turning off the TV. He didn't feel like fighting any more. He wanted to go to sleep and forget everything. His tired body was asking for rest. He would think about it tomorrow.

Facing the World

Emilio let the rain fall freely on his head as he walked to school. It felt good. It seemed to calm his nerves. His mother had made sure he left with enough time so he wouldn't be late.

He tried not to attract attention. His knees shook as he stood in front of his classroom door. I can't do this. I'm going home, he thought. No, he wasn't a coward. His papa wouldn't have liked it. He had to face the world. "Papa, help me. I just don't know what to do," he said softly.

"Good morning, Emilio. I'm glad you're on time today. Were you sick yesterday?" asked the teacher as Emilio tried to sneak quietly to the back of the room—his favorite place.

José stood up and looked at Emilio accusingly, but just translated what the teacher had said.

"I've an excuse. Here it is," said Emilio, pulling the piece of paper out of one of his books.

The teacher handed the paper to José to translate. At that moment Emilio made up his mind to learn English even if he didn't do anything else in his life. He wouldn't put himself in José's, or anybody else's, hands any longer. His mother was right about being a victim. There was no way to know if Jose had translated the excuse or made up his own.

"Sit down," said the teacher, without referring to the paper in her hand.

Emilio saw José intently looking at him. He avoided his eyes and tried to concentrate on what the teacher was saying. He understood some words and even short sentences. Watching TV and listening to people had helped him understand words he heard often.

Recess came sooner than Emilio wanted. He managed to duck José, who had tried to corner him twice. It wasn't going to be easy to continue to avoid everyone for the rest of the day. He waited for his classmates to leave before he ventured out of the building, hoping to stay out of sight.

"¿Qué se hizo ayer? Where did you go? Were you afraid to come out with your wet pants?" asked José, coming from behind. "You didn't want us to see you. Well, I did, and all of us know you wet your pants, right?" José looked at the group gathering around them and mockingly repeated the words from the paper he had translated earlier. "*My son had a problem on his way to school, ha, ha, ha.*"

"Yes, we know about your wet pants," said someone.

"What are you talking about? I didn't come to school yesterday, and that's that." The words came to Emilio as if they had been given to him by the Holy Spirit. There were times when people had to fib, even God permitted it, he hoped.

"You know I saw you in the bathroom. I bet you sneaked out of school and went back home, but don't tell me I didn't see you," said José, annoyed.

"I don't know who you saw, but it wasn't me." Emilio could hardly believe he was talking so calmly.

"Emilio, where have you been? I looked for you yesterday," said Clara, smiling.

The voice startled Emilio. How could she smile after what he did to her? She invited him to meet her friends and have a nice day with them at the game, and he had disappeared without saying goodbye.

"I didn't come to school yesterday," said Emilio, lowering his head.

"He came, I saw him, really, I did. He managed to leave because he wet his pants," said José in a loud voice.

"Why don't you ask the principal to lend you a microphone so you can tell the school that you saw Emilio—who was not even here—with wet pants," said Clara.

"Who called you? You're always where you aren't wanted." José gave Clara a mean look.

"I have as much right to be here as you. You're angry because I don't believe you. I'll make sure no one else does."

"Do you think anyone is going to pay attention to a silly girl who is always defending every stupid kid in school?" José's dark eyes shone with rage.

"I don't believe you *either*," said Ali, coming out of nowhere.

Emilio looked at them, mesmerized. He had never expected anyone to come to his aid. What kind of person was Clara? Why was she still helping him? It took him a few seconds to even recognize Ali.

"Who cares if you believe me or not? Who are you, anyway?" asked José.

"I'm Emilio's friend," answered the thin, wide-eyed boy.

Emilio felt bad for not remembering Ali. The boy's reply, in broken Spanish, touched him. He then recalled Clara talking about someone from Jordan and remembered the boy talking to him before he left the stadium. How did he speak Spanish? This thought flashed through his mind so fast he forgot it immediately.

"Come, Emilio, Pablo and Marcia are waiting for us. You don't have to stay here." Clara pulled him by the arm.

"You're a stinky coward," shouted José as Clara, Emilio and Ali walked away.

"You're a creep!" yelled Emilio.

The shouting voices followed until they merged with the rest of the noise, in a loud roar.

"Gracias, Clara, and you too, Ali. I'm sorry I left the game the other day. I thought you were

feeling sorry for me and I didn't like it. I still think you do," said Emilio.

"What's wrong with that?" asked Clara.

"I don't like to be 'poor Emilio.' I don't want you to be my friends just because you feel sorry for me. It only makes me feel worse." Emilio kept surprising himself by talking candidly. It was something he didn't do often.

"Emilio, we like you, but we also feel sorry for you since almost everyone in the class picks on you. We want to help you. As long as they think you're alone and helpless they'll torment you."

"I'm glad you like me, but I still don't like you to feel sorry for me. Thank you for helping me."

"We do like you, believe me," said Clara. "What really happened to you yesterday? I didn't believe José's story about you wetting your pants. How ridiculous!"

Emilio had again the desire to run away from this friendly group. They believed in him even when he was lying. He wished he didn't have to lie, but he couldn't tell the truth. How could he? Emilio felt his face grow hot. It would only be a matter of minutes before they would read the truth on his face. His mind was working hard to come up with an excuse.

"I fell down on my way to school and I had to go back home." It was the best he could do, since his mother had written something happening on his way to school.

"Did you hurt yourself?" asked Ali in his broken Spanish.

"Not really, but I tore my pants and I had to go home." Emilio dreaded going through this moment. "Anyway, I didn't come to school. I also felt bad about you, since I left the game the way I did. I didn't know what to tell you. I'm sorry."

"It's okay. Let's don't talk about it. You'll go with us to the next game. It's almost time to go back to class," said Clara, as they walked back to the building.

Marcia, followed by her brother Pablo, walked toward them. "We have been waiting for you," she said.

"Emilio was having a hard time with José and Cato. It took a little while to get him out of their paws," said Clara. "I forgot about you, sorry."

"Hola, where have you been hiding?" asked Pablo, giving Emilio a friendly smile.

Emilio didn't feel like going through the whole thing again. *"Hola,"* he said, not answering the question.

The sound of the bell put a stop to the conversation. Emilio hoped his friends and enemies would forget his not being in school the day before, and his leaving the game, so he could go on with his life.

"So I heard you wet your pants. I would have given anything to have seen you. Only a stupid boy like you would wet his pants at your age," said Matt in English as they walked back to the school building.

"What did he say?" Emilio asked Clara.

"Something about you wetting your pants. Don't pay attention to him. You know he just wants to give you a hard time." Clara kept on walking. Matt, followed by Cato, kept on shouting something in English.

"Don't look at them. The more you argue with them, the worse they behave. Believe me, I know. Ignore them," said Marcia.

It took every bit of willpower Emilio possessed to keep from jumping on the kid who had made it his pastime to make his life miserable. He wanted to hit Matt's big, plump body until he had emptied out all his resentment. He didn't say anything to anybody. He would explode if he did.

"Run, coward, run," yelled Cato.

"Play deaf, Emilio. You'll soon find a way to stand up to them. We're here for you," said Clara, smiling more prettily than ever.

"Gracias." Emilio couldn't say anything else. He had a knot in his throat. Clara and her friends were okay after all.

A New Experience

"I can't believe I'm talking to you in English," said Ali one afternoon soon after as he and Emilio left together after school. "Now I'll have to find someone else to help me practice Spanish."

"You can practice with me anytime," said Emilio in Spanish. "I speak bad English, don't I?" he asked, going back to English. "But it sure beats not being able to talk or understand people."

"I think you do real good. A couple of months ago you barely knew a few words."

"I had to learn to survive, but it has been hard for me. I'm not like you, speaking four languages. How you learned them so good?" Emilio would be happy enough to do well in Spanish and get along in English.

"I guess you're right about having the knack for learning certain subjects," said Ali. "I had to learn English when I came to this country three years ago, and I've been taking Spanish in school too. I like languages, but other things I'm not so good at, like math. Do you need help with your homework?" asked Ali, changing the subject.

"We don't have much for tomorrow, but it's fun to do homework together. I'm glad you wanted to help me," said Emilio, grateful for what Ali had done for him.

In just a few weeks the two boys had become best friends. They seemed to have a lot in common. They even looked alike, small and thin—even their skin color was similar. Every day after school they had gone to the public library to study. Ali tutored Emilio until he could speak and understand English passably.

"I wish I knew what I was good at, so I could be the best at something. Even my brother Jaime, who doesn't like school and says he'll leave as soon as he's sixteen, is good at *looking* good, and he has lots of friends. Every person is good at something, according to Mama." Emilio often wondered why he had come into this world short of whatever special something it was that other people had.

"You're good with numbers, and I think you're more than an okay guy," said Ali. "Let's go to my house for a while. After we finish our homework we can watch TV. I'll give you a piece of real Arab bread my mother made this morning."

The invitation surprised Emilio. The two boys had kept away from each other's homes. Emilio didn't think his family would like Ali. He didn't know why. It was just a gut feeling. Everyone seemed to feel funny about people from other countries, distrustful of them.

"I've got to be home by five," said Emilio. "Jaime gets upset with me when I don't go home after school. He has to stay in until Mama comes home from work, and he doesn't like to play with Victoria. She also gets mad with me if I'm not there. She and Jaime fight all the time."

"We have a couple of hours, so let's go," said Ali, eagerly.

"What about your family?" Emilio felt uneasy about going to his friend's house. Surely his family would be very different.

"My mother said it would be okay to invite you. She wants to meet you," said Ali.

"Está bien, I'll call Jaime from your house," said Emilio, uneasily. What if Ali's mother didn't like him? Would she be weird? Why did he need to go there? He had to put up with too many people he could hardly understand in English to go to another place he might not be welcome.

"On second thought, maybe I shouldn't. Mama doesn't like me to go places where she doesn't know the people," said Emilio, suddenly using the best excuse he could find.

"A second ago you said you were going. Why did you change your mind? I thought you were my friend. You went to Clara's house last week."

"We all met there before going to the last game," said Emilio. "We didn't stay more than fifteen minutes."

Emilio had been uneasy the day he went to Clara's house, but somehow he knew her family would be like his. They were the same kind of people. He was right: Clara's mother looked a lot like Herminia. Her older sister was pretty, and Jaime would have loved to meet her. He was crazy about pretty girls.

"Okay, I'll go." Emilio couldn't disappoint his friend. Ali had helped him to keep Matt, Cato, and José at arm's length, even though they still didn't waste any opportunity to make fun of him.

The boys walked quietly toward Ali's house, about six blocks away from Emilio's. Ali looked hurt by their conversation. Emilio felt bad. The wide-eyed boy, along with Pablo, Marcia and Clara, had made his life easier and happier.

"Mama, Mama!" yelled Ali as he walked into an old, small house, with Emilio almost hiding behind him.

A cascade of words Emilio could not make out poured from a woman with eyes as dark and as big as her son's. She embraced Ali and kissed him on both cheeks, and before Emilio knew it she was also hugging and kissing him. Embarrassment made him so tense that every muscle in his body stiffened. He felt the white shawl the woman had around her head, rubbing against his face. Emilio didn't know what to think.

"Mama doesn't speak much English," said Ali after his mother left the room. The boys sat on an old sofa. "She's going to bring us bread and tea. I hope you like it."

"Tea?" asked Emilio. It was not a drink he was

used to having. He had heard his mother talking about the tea parties held by the high-class society in his home country, but he had no idea what a tea party actually was. He figured that tea must be so special he was not allowed to drink it.

"What's wrong with tea?" asked Ali, looking at Emilio in a strange way.

"Nothing . . . I'm sure I'll like it." Emilio felt as if he had entered another world, a world he didn't know, making him very uncomfortable.

"You look nervous. Are you afraid of something?" asked Ali.

"No, of course not. It's just—" Emilio couldn't put into words what he was feeling. He didn't understand it himself. "Don't mind me. I'm always nervous when I go to places I don't know. I'm fine."

"I thought you'd be different. I can't believe you, of all people, would think we are weird." Ali looked as if he were going to cry.

"I—I didn't—" Emilio couldn't believe himself. Was he doing to Ali what others had done to him? "I'm sorry. I would never . . . I'm glad to be here, really. Let's start doing our homework, okay?"

"Okay," said Ali, still pouting.

The boys took their books and notebooks out of their knapsacks and worked in silence for a while. Ali's mother came back, carrying a tray. Again a torrent of strange words poured from her mouth. She treated them as if they were special creatures she had to tend to. She was still talking even as she walked away.

"This is delicious," said Emilio, munching on a piece of bread that looked like an overgrown, thick tortilla.

"Do you like it?" asked Ali.

"Yes, I do, and it's still warm. Do you eat this bread all the time?" Emilio grabbed another piece.

"Every day, with every meal. It's like tortilla for you or wheat bread for others. Here, try it with tea," said Ali, handing Emilio a cup of tea his mother had poured before she left.

Emilio took a sip from the cup. The strange taste of the beverage made him gag for a second. He held the liquid inside his mouth briefly, then gulped it down. It was insipid, like the herb water his mother used to give him when he was sick. He put the cup down and ate a piece of bread to kill the taste in his mouth.

"You didn't like it, right?" asked Ali, observing Emilio.

"Why do you say that?"

"You made a face," said Ali.

"I love the bread, but the tea tastes so different," said Emilio, wondering what he was going to do with the rest of the tea. He wasn't planning to drink it.

The boys watched television for a while. Ali's mother came back, said something to Emilio, took the cup of cold tea, made a face of distaste, went to the kitchen, and came back with a fresh cup of hot tea.

"Thank you," said Emilio, a faint smile on his face.

Still talking and smiling, Ali's mother left the room again.

"You didn't drink your tea, so Mama brought you a fresh cup," said Ali.

"I'll drink it." Emilio took the cup to his mouth. "I've got to go now. Ali." Emilio got up and gathered his papers. "Can I have a glass of water?"

"Sure, I'll get it." Ali ran to the kitchen.

Emilio took his cup, rushed to the front door, opened it and poured the liquid outdoors.

"What were you doing?" asked Ali, holding a glass, half-filled with water.

"I was looking to see if it was getting dark. I finished my tea," he said, putting the cup on the coffee table. "I better go now. I'll see you tomorrow in school."

"Don't you want your water?"

"Sure," said Emilio, drinking the whole glass.

"I'll walk with you to the corner. Let's go." Ali opened the front door.

"Well, wouldn't you know? We got them both in one place," yelled Matt's unmistakable voice. They had walked about a block from Ali's house.

Emilio froze. What was Matt doing there? In an almost involuntary reflex, he moved his hands up as if to stop something or somebody from hitting him.

"Cato, you take the other one, leave this stupid kid, what's-his-name, to me," shouted Matt.

"Cowards, why don't you pick on somebody your own size? Do you think that hitting us makes you better?" asked Ali, in a quivering voice.

Emilio didn't say a word He closed his eyes and waited for the worst.

Encounters

"Did you think you could avoid us forever?" asked Cato, sarcastically. "You've been *bad*, very *bad*."

"Yeah!" yelled Matt, hitting Emilio. "No one messes with us. You two don't belong here. Go back to where you came from, worms!"

Ali and Emilio, taken by surprise, seemed to have lost their speech and their ability to react. Matt continued to hit Emilio. But when Cato did the same to Ali, the boy suddenly got his voice back and began to scream hoarsely.

"Stop screaming!" yelled Cato.

"You're mean, envious, and stupid, and Matt is *fat* and stupid," said Ali, regaining some calm.

"You call me stupid?" Cato hit Ali so hard the boy fell backwards and hit his head against the sidewalk.

"What did he say?" Matt reddened with anger. He hurled another punch into Emilio's face, then jumped on Ali as the boy hit the ground.

Emilio wobbled on his feet but he didn't fall. He had avoided some of the punches by dodging around his assailant.

"Don't hit him. He's—" said Cato, pulling Matt off of Ali, who was not moving.

"What did you do to him? *¡Dios mío!*"

screamed Emilio.

"Let's get out of here," said Cato, running away so fast Emilio hardly saw him disappear. Matt followed as quickly as his overweight body permitted.

"Ali, are you okay?" Emilio kneeled by his friend, shaking him by the arm.

"Ouch, my head," mumbled Ali, as he opened his eyes and tried to get up.

"What possessed you to say those things to them? You know they are mean and so much bigger than we are." Emilio didn't know what to think. His friend was either very brave or very foolish.

"Help me get up," said Ali, trying to push himself up. He held his head with his right hand. "Woo, I have a big bump here, look!"

"You sure do," said Emilio touching the protruding part of Ali's head. "I'll help you walk back to your house. Better go slow. Do you think you'll have to go to the doctor?"

"I don't know. I don't want to. They always give you shots." Ali stumbled.

With unsteady steps the boys returned to the house they had left just minutes before. Ali's mother came to the door. Her eyes grew even larger—if that was possible—at seeing her son, and listening to his explanation in her native tongue.

"I hope you feel better, I'm sorry they hurt you.

I'll see you tomorrow." Emilio didn't want to go back inside the house, as Ali's mother motioned at him to do. "Bye," he said rushing away.

Emilio could still hear Ali's mother fussing as he reached the corner.

"What took you so long?" asked Jaime as his brother walked in the door. "Victoria is crying in Mama's room because I didn't want to play a circus clown. I just don't have patience to do every silly thing she makes up."

"You don't have patience with anybody. All you want to do is to go out with your friends. No one in this house matters to you, not even Mama." Emilio was in no mood to hear his brother's complaints. "You're not the only person here wanting to go out and do things. Wasn't that what you wanted me to do? To go out and make some friends? Now you're sore because I'm not home to play with Victoria."

"It isn't fun to sit here every afternoon babysitting kids," Jaime said. "I think you're old enough to do it sometimes. I'm going to talk to Mama about it. You're better with her anyway." Jaime put down the notebook he held and paced in front of Emilio.

"Do whatever you want. I'm going to see about Victoria."

Emilio was now feeling the effects of the beating. He had been so fearful while walking home that Matt and Cato would appear again that he didn't realize his body was hurting everywhere. His face felt hot from the punches. Nothing seemed to be broken, though. Still, he had to find a way to stop Matt and Cato from harassing him. Emilio knew he couldn't win a fistfight; his size and strength were no match for them. He had to think of a more creative solution.

"What's your problem, Victoria?" asked Emilio, entering his mother's room as he pushed aside his thoughts.

"Jaime is so mean. He doesn't like to do anything I ask him. He is always sending me to my room. I don't like him," said Victoria, whimpering. She sat on her mother's bed, holding a rag doll.

"You've got to entertain yourself sometimes. Jaime isn't the same as before, so you better not bother him." Emilio said this more to himself than to his sister. He missed his older brother, the boy he used to play with before he became a teenager with more important things to do. Emilio smiled at her. "People grow up and change."

Brother and sister spent the next hour drawing pictures Victoria needed for school the next day. They heard their mother in the kitchen but didn't stop what they were doing, which was unusual, especially for Victoria, who always waited eagerly for her mother's return.

"Emilio, I need you to go to the store to get a

couple of tomatoes," said Herminia, entering the room.

"Why doesn't Jaime go? He never does anything around here," said Emilio.

"He takes care of you," said Herminia in a strange tone of voice, as if apologizing. "Besides, he's not here. He left a few minutes ago."

"You let him do anything he wants."

"Jaime was mean, Mama," interrupted Victoria. "Tell him to play with me sometimes."

"Está bien, hija," said Herminia. "Emilio, don't start with that again. I do the best I can with all of you. When you get to be Jaime's age you'll have the same privileges. Now, go get those tomatoes for me. I need them for dinner."

Reluctantly, Emilio took the money his mother handed him and left to go to the convenience store, three blocks from his home. It was still daylight. It was the end of April and the days were getting longer and warmer.

Emilio walked fast, still afraid of encountering Matt, Cato, or even José, who lived close by. He hurried, looking around and making sure no one was following him. He bought two plump tomatoes and headed back home.

As he came out of the store he saw a group of about six older boys, all wearing bandannas on their heads. Emilio immediately retreated and hid behind a telephone booth outside the store. He waited for them to go away. Who were they?

Were his enemies among them? The group began to walk, dangerously close, towards where Emilio hid.

"Los Alacranes are going to do something tonight," said a stocky boy. "They found out who painted their front doors last week. We have to be careful."

"They better not mess around with us," said another.

The familiar voice caught Emilio's attention. He moved his head a few inches outside the wall of the telephone booth so he could see the person talking. What was Jaime doing there? Why was he wearing a bandanna? Was his brother in some kind of *pandilla*? Was that the reason he was out until after ten every evening? Emilio didn't know what to think. His confused mind wouldn't work. The group crossed the street and disappeared from his sight.

Too many things were happening around him. What was he to do? He didn't want his brother to get hurt. Should he tell his mother? *Papa, why aren't you here? I can't do this by myself.*

Emilio ran back home, gave the tomatoes to his mother and went to his room. He hardly ate that evening, tormented by the discovery of his brother's activities, and dreading having to go to school tomorrow.

The Next Day

The dream he'd had the night before seemed so real that now Emilio sat in the classroom with his eyes closed, reliving the scenes.

Every detail came rushing to his mind. He saw Jaime and himself, walking with their father by the cornfield, early in the morning, as they did so many mornings.

"Jaime, I want you to take Emilio to town this afternoon and show him where to buy supplies. Don't forget to get enough rope to tie the mule. The old one broke. It's time Emilio learns where things are. You're the oldest and should be the one guiding the others," said his Papa, repeating what he had often said to Jaime.

There was something about the oldest child in a family Emilio never understood. What about the other children? Were they born different? It didn't seem right that the oldest was always better and wiser. Would he never reach an age when he would be wiser and older than his brother.?

"Papa, tell Jaime he can't be a *pandillero,* because I don't want to be one. Am I supposed to do everything he does? What should I be when I grow up?" Emilio asked his father, who didn't answer. His papa looked at him so tenderly, Emilio threw himself in his arms and cried.

"Emilio. Emilio!" called the teacher. "Why don't you join the rest of the class? You need to keep on top of things to stay up with the others."

"I'm sorry. I was–" Emilio opened his eyes. He realized his classmates were looking at him as if he had done something wrong.

"I want you to stand up and read, slowly and clearly, the passage about the writing of our Constitution," ordered the teacher.

Emilio was strangely grateful that no one else his age attended this particular class. He had been put in a lower-level history class because he had not taken American History before. It took Emilio a few seconds to shake off the dream that had lingered through the waking hours of the morning. He concentrated on the page he was reading, stumbling over some of the long words he found difficult to pronounce. He managed to finish reading a page and half before the teacher asked him to stop.

"You're improving Emilio, but you need to stop daydreaming and pay more attention."

"Yes, ma'am." Emilio hated to be called in class. He knew his classmates laughed whenever he mispronounced a word, which happened most of the time. He now saw the bilingual teacher only when he needed special help.

Emilio was eager for the class to be over so he could find out about Ali. He hadn't seen him yet. Emilio hoped the bump on Ali's head was gone, and he wished that Matt, Cato, and José would vanish. He dreaded meeting them.

"Emilio, I've been looking for you," cried out Clara as he walked outside the building during recess.

"Don't shout like that, Clara," said Emilio, annoyed.

"Well, sorry! What's the matter?" Clara looked hurt.

"I'm sorry, Clara, I didn't meant to snap at you. Matt and Cato beat up Ali and me yesterday, and I don't want to bump into them."

"They beat you up? I think we should tell the principal. Did they hurt you?" Clara looked at him in a strange way.

"No, it would be worse if we tell on them. They would never leave me alone if they get punished because of me. I think I know how to solve the problem with them. It's going to take me a while but I know how to show them. I have a plan." The idea thrilled Emilio. It had landed in his mind so suddenly, he again credited the Holy Spirit for it.

"What are you talking about?" asked Clara.

"You have to wait and see. What did you want to tell me?" asked Emilio.

"You remember my friend Kathy, the girl with red hair who went with us to the baseball game?" Clara's eyes were bright with excitement.

"Of course, I remember her. Why?" asked Emilio intrigued.

"Her birthday is next week and she asked me to invite you for next Saturday," said Clara. "We're going ice-skating at the Galleria, and then we'll go on to one of the restaurants for cake and ice cream. I'm so excited. Isn't it wonderful? I told you that things would get better."

"She's inviting me to the Galleria? Are you sure?" asked Emilio in disbelief.

"Yes, she wants you to go. She likes you. Pablo, Marcia, Ali, you and I, and a couple of friends from her class are invited."

"I don't know how to ice-skate." Emilio couldn't see himself in such a place. He never dreamed he would be going to that kind of party. Were Kathy's parents rich? The invitation overwhelmed him.

"I don't know either, but we can learn. It'll be a lot of fun. I can't wait." Clara turned serious. "Now tell me about yesterday."

"You know how Cato, Matt, and José have been waiting for an opportunity to get back at me. Well, they did." Emilio told Clara what had happened the day before.

"I'm okay, but I'm getting worried about Ali though." Emilio looked around in search of his friend. "I haven't seen him today. I want to find him before we go back inside."

"Okay, *vamos*," said Clara.

Ali was nowhere. Clara asked a girl who took several classes with their friend if she had seen him, but she said she had not.

"Look! There is Cato, talking to José," exclaimed Clara as they prepared to give up the search.

Emilio's first reaction was to run in the opposite direction. He then remembered what his mother had said to him, which was still embedded in his brain, "Don't play victim." He decided to stay where he was. Cato pretended not to see him, but Emilio could tell he was aware of his and Clara's presence.

"I won't let them frighten me any more," said Emilio to himself, filled with a determination and self-confidence he didn't know he had. "I wonder why José wasn't with Matt and Cato yesterday." The question popped into his brain at seeing José walking toward them, and he blurted it out loud.

"I don't think he is as bad as the other two. He just wants to be a big shot like them," said Clara. "I have to go get a book from my locker. I'll go with you this afternoon to Ali's house to find out what happened."

"I hope he's all right."

As they walked back to the building Emilio saw Matt coming from the left. Seeing Clara and Emilio, Matt stopped abruptly, lowered his eyes, and backtracked.

"Why did he do that?" asked Emilio.

"Didn't you say he and Cato pushed Ali down and left? I bet they are afraid they hurt Ali. That's the only explanation for acting weird," said Clara.

"Sí, that must be it."

"I've to get that book. See you after school," said Clara leaving Emilio at the entrance.

"Aren't you happy you can understand people now? I'm sure glad I don't have to translate for you any more," said José in English, catching up with Emilio.

"Yes, I'm very glad. I don't like to depend on other people," said Emilio in the best English he could manage. Why was José talking to him? He never talked to him before, unless he was translating something for him, or making fun of him.

"Didn't I see you with Clara just now?" asked José in an unusually polite voice. "Where is she?"

"She went ahead to her class. I have to go now." Emilio didn't feel like talking to this boy who had ridiculed him.

"By the way it has been a while since I saw your friend . . . What's his name? Ali? Yeah, I think that's his name. Is he sick or something?" José seemed to be looking for the right words to ask about Ali.

"What is it to you? It's not as if you care, right?" *Yes, they were afraid to get in trouble,* thought Emilio. He was sure Matt and Cato had sent José over to ask him about Ali.

"I don't know why he didn't come to school. Why don't you ask your friends? I see them there waiting for you. Ask them about what they did to

Ali and me yesterday. They hurt Ali." It felt good to leave them in suspense. Emilio left José standing at the entrance and rushed inside.

The rest of the day went by slowly. Emilio was uneasy and apprehensive. His three enemies avoided crossing paths with him. They glanced at him at lunch but they didn't approach him. The situation gave Emilio something of an advantage he wasn't going to waste.

Clara and Emilio went by Ali's house after school. His mother had kept the boy home. She had taken him to the doctor, who said Ali had a mild concussion. They visited with him for a while. Emilio, feeling much better about his friend, continued brewing a plan. There were actually two plans: one to keep his enemies in suspense about Ali, and another that had begun to take form in his mind. "Well, one thing at a time," he said to himself as he walked back home, after accompanying Clara to her house.

Learning to Ice-Skate

"Why were you hanging around a bunch of strange-looking boys, and wearing a bandanna on your head?" asked Emilio when his brother came into the room late the following night. "They are older than you, and they look *mean*."

"What boys? What are you talking about?" Jaime seemed subdued as he sat on his bed.

"Don't play dumb with me. I saw you yesterday when Mama sent me to the store. Are you a *pandillero?* Papa wouldn't have liked that. The teachers in my school tell us about the horrible things gangs do in cities all over this country. Is that true?" Gangs horrified Emilio, and yet the idea of belonging to one attracted him. It seemed exciting and grown-up. But . . . he knew better.

"Who told you they were a gang? For your information we're not a *pandilla.* We just like to hang around together. We're friends," said Jaime, taking his shoes and pants off. He put on an old T-shirt and a pair of wrinkled shorts and slipped under the cover.

"Why would you wear bandannas and talk about doing crazy stuff then?" asked Emilio.

"It's no big deal. We like to be silly sometimes. Go to sleep and leave me alone." Jaime turned the light off. "Now, don't go telling Mama lies about me."

"Gangs are dangerous. I don't want anything happening to you," said Emilio.

"We don't do anything dangerous. Me and my friends have fun doing stuff. That's all. Forget it and let me sleep."

"Okay, but remember Papa always said you're to teach us, me and Victoria. We don't want to do bad things." Emilio waited for his brother to comment but Jaime ignored him.

He soon forgot Jaime and his friends, promising himself to spy on them again. Something exciting was happening to *him* for a change: Emilio was going to the Galleria with his friends.

He couldn't imagine such a place. He had heard people talk about the big mall with its ice-skating rink and fancy stores. For Emilio it was a place for rich people, not for him. Even so, Emilio went to sleep with a smile on his face.

The days went by slowly while Emilio waited in expectation. He kept Matt and his friends anxious about Ali's health after the beating. They didn't care about Ali, but they worried they would held accountable for what they'd done. Anyway, he didn't want to think about them now. Kathy's party was such a big event that Emilio didn't know what to do with himself. He was nervous, and at times he feared going.

"Can I go with you?" Victoria asked, a pitiful look on her face. "My friend Minerva went with her mother one day. She said the Galleria was the prettiest place in the whole world."

"I've told you you can't go. Kathy invited me, not you. Besides, you're too young for this party," said Emilio, combing his hair.

Joy and fear made him jittery. He had taken a shower and put on his best outfit, a white shirt he inherited from Jaime, and a pair of khaki pants his mother had bought when he started school.

"No one takes me anywhere. You're all mean. I don't like you." Victoria left her brother's room in a huff.

Emilio finished combing his hair for the fifth time and walked out of the room. "Mama, did you wrap the present?"

"It's on the kitchen table," yelled Herminia from somewhere.

"I'll see you later, Mama," shouted Emilio, grabbing the wrapped book he had bought at the bookstore. His mother wanted him to buy something that would make him look good. It had a pretty blue cover and a fancy title he couldn't pronounce.

"Let me see you," said Herminia, leaving what she was doing to inspect the boy. "You look handsome, son. See, you can look good if you want to." She turned him around twice before she let him go. "Remember to be polite, say thank you and—"

Emilio didn't hear the rest; he was already out of the apartment, rushing down the stairs. He had to hurry before he changed his mind and went back to his haven.

Several times Emilio backtracked his steps but continued on. He was meeting Ali at Clara's house. The three of them were going to Kathy's. He struggled with his fears until he found himself knocking at the door of his friend's house.

"Are you excited? I am," said Clara, looking so pretty that Emilio's mouth hung open.

"Of course I am." Emilio could not take his eyes away from the girl who had been like his guardian angel since they met. She wore white pants and a bright red blouse with ruffles. Her long hair shone so beautifully, Emilio wanted to touch it, but he wouldn't dare.

"What's the matter with you, Emilio? You look weird," said Clara.

"Nothing." Emilio blushed. He felt his face turned hot. "Where is Ali?"

"He should have arrived by now. I hope he gets here soon, we need to leave in about five minutes. I'll go inside and get the present. We'll wait for Ali here." Clara went into the house, coming right out again carrying a small package in her hand.

"There he comes," said Emilio as he spotted Ali.

The trio walked in silence to Kathy's house, less than a block away. They didn't seem able to put their feelings into words. A few minutes later Emilio found himself inside a van driven by

Kathy's mother, along with a lot of kids, mostly girls. Everything was a blur to him. He had no idea how long it took them to arrive at the most beautiful place he had ever seen, not counting the countryside and mountains outside Conchagua.

"Stay together. I don't want to lose anyone," said Kathy's mother who looked just like her daughter, with the same red, wild hair and freckled face.

Emilio followed the group like a robot while they made their way to where they were going. His eyes were not big enough to take in everything around him.

"Do you like it?" asked Clara, giggling.

"Sí, it's beautiful," mumbled Emilio, his eyes fixed on the ice rink.

"You're afraid of the ice, right?" asked Clara. "Don't worry, if those kids down there can do it, I don't see why we can't." She seemed to be reassuring herself.

Kathy's mother stopped in front of the rink's entrance. "Wait here until I get the tickets. Then go downstairs and put on your skates."

Emilio hated being so ignorant. He didn't know how to do anything. He couldn't ride a bicycle since he had never owned one. Ice-skating was not even in his vocabulary.

The last thing he remembered he was putting on the skates and then he found himself on the ice, holding on to the wall. He planned to stay there for as long as he could.

"Don't look so scared; it's embarrassing," said Clara, also grabbing onto the wall. "I don't know how to skate either, but I hope I don't look that frightened."

"I can't help it. How can anybody keep the balance on top of two blades?" Emilio looked at dozens of people gliding over the ice and twirling around and around as if they were made out of rubber.

"How are you doing?" asked a man, approaching them.

"We don't know how to skate," said Clara.

"I'll be glad to help you. My name is Tom and I work here. Let's go. Put your right foot forward and let me guide you," he said, taking Clara along. "I'll be back for you."

Emilio didn't say anything. He looked at the pair, moving among the skaters. Clara seemed reluctant but kept on trying to skate. She stumbled several times before she seemed to go along with what Tom tried to teach her. Emilio dreaded having to venture away from the wall. He still had time to walk back and wait for the others on firmer ground.

"Where are you going?" asked Ali, skating to where Emilio was.

"I'm going to wait outside. I can't do this." Emilio wanted to get out of there as fast as he could.

"You're giving up before you even try?"

"I'm not like you. You can do everything. When did you learn to skate? Did you know how to do it before you came to Houston?" asked Emilio.

"I lived in New York for a year. I learned there. It's not difficult if you relax and let yourself slide. Look at me." Ali demonstrated his abilities, skating in front of Emilio.

"Ready?" asked Tom, taking Emilio by the arm. He had been so engrossed in what Ali was doing he hadn't seen Tom come back.

"No, I'm not ready. I'm getting out of here."

"You wouldn't like waiting out there. Come on," said Tom, softly pushing the boy away from the wall before he could do anything.

"Go, Emilio, *go!*" yelled Ali.

Emilio knew he would fall and break his neck, a leg, or maybe every bone in his body. He grabbed Tom's arm. "Let me go. I'm leaving this place." He could hardly stand the fear.

Tom didn't acknowledge his pleas. "Look at my feet and try to do the same. Put your right foot first and then your left foot." Tom went on, instructing Emilio and guiding him.

"You can do it, Emilio," he heard someone say. He didn't look. He needed all the concentration he could gather.

After the third time around the rink Emilio was getting the knack of it. He felt more at ease.

"You were a difficult one, but you've got it. Good luck," said Tom skating away, leaving Emilio in the middle of the rink. "Don't let go. Continue skating."

Emilio panicked. How was he going to get out of there? He stumbled but didn't fall, managing to go on moving, almost inadvertently, filling his lungs with the air that hit him as he gained speed.

It was as if another person had entered his body. What a wonderful feeling, a feeling of freedom, of power, of something so thrilling Emilio could not identify. He went around and around as if he had wings. His agile body, free of fear, moved over the ice as if it had been born on it.

"Didn't I tell you? I was right," said Clara, catching up with him. "You're better than me. I just barely keep myself from falling. But, look at you. I'm impressed."

"Thank you," said Emilio, slowing down. "I can't explain it, Clara. This is a miracle. Come with me."

Clara and Emilio skated without stopping for a long time.

"You seem to be enjoying yourselves," said Kathy, joining them. "Emilio, I thought you said you didn't know how to skate."

He smiled, proudly. "I didn't, really, I had never skated before. You don't know how scared I was. It just happened."

"I'm glad it did. I'm also glad you learned how to speak English. It makes it easier for me to talk to you. I like that," said Kathy. "It's time to go eat cake and ice cream."

"Can I go around one more time?" asked Emilio.

"Yes, another round. It won't take but a minute," said Clara.

"Okay, but hurry. Mama is already at the restaurant waiting for us. I'll see you outside, I have got to go get the others." Kathy skated away.

They had cake and ice cream, talked and laughed. Emilio enjoyed himself for the first time since his father died and his life changed forever.

It was getting dark when Emilio returned home after a day he would never forget. Herminia met him at the door.

"Emilio, *hijo,* I'm glad you're here. *¡Dios mío!* It has to be a mistake." She fell into a chair. "It's a mistake!" she exclaimed, holding her head in her hands as she got up again.

"¿Qué pasa, Mama?" A cold feeling came over Emilio.

"The police just called. They said Jaime is in jail. But why would Jaime be in jail? You stay here with Victoria. I know this is a mistake." Herminia kept repeating the last sentence until she was out of the apartment.

Emilio's heart sank. This was not the way he

expected the day to end. What had Jaime done? He should have told his mother about Jaime and the *pandilla.* Why hadn't he? *Papa, don't let anything happen to my brother. Talk to God, please.*

Hard Times

"Emilio, Emilio, get up, go to your room," said Herminia in a quivering voice. Emilio had waited so long for his mother that he had finally fallen asleep on the sofa.

"What? Mama? What time is it? Where is Jaime?" Emilio awoke with a heavy heart. It took him a moment to remember why he was here instead of in his bed.

"It's almost midnight. I couldn't bring him home. What am I going to do?" Herminia sat down and cried. She looked small and helpless.

"What happened, Mama? Why is Jaime in jail?"

"The police said he was a *pandillero.* They believe his gang vandalized the high school and stole money from the cafeteria. Jaime couldn't have done something like that. He's a good boy," said Herminia, sobbing.

"Did you see him? What did he tell you?"

"They let me see him for a few minutes. He kept on saying 'I'm sorry, Mama.' He didn't answer any of my questions. *Mi pobre hijo, Dios mío ayúdanos."* Herminia put her hands together and prayed. "I begged, pleaded, and tried everything, but they wouldn't let him come home."

A feeling of helplessness settled in his being. "It's true, Mama, Jaime was hanging around with a gang. I saw him the other day when you sent me to the store. He was with a bunch of boys, wearing bandannas. I was afraid to tell you. I didn't want Jaime to be mad at me. He was already weird with me. We should call *tío* Pedro to help us get him out of jail."

"Sí, claro," said Herminia. "Why didn't I think of Pedro before. Your uncle will know what to do." Herminia stood up, ready to fight. "Just because Jaime was hanging around with those kids doesn't mean he is stealing like them." She went to the telephone, picked up the receiver, and paused for a moment. "I guess it's too late to call. I'll do it first thing in the morning. Is Victoria asleep?"

"Yes, she went to bed about nine. I didn't tell her about Jaime. She wanted to wait for you, but I told her you and Jaime were working at the store." Emilio wanted to go to bed. He didn't like acting like a grown-up, thinking about things he didn't quite understand.

"I need to rest. *Una taza de agua de toronjil* will help me sleep. Herb tea is very good for the nerves." Herminia seemed to be talking to herself. "Go to bed, *hijo,*" she said as she walked to the kitchen.

It took three days for *tío* Pedro to get Jaime

out of jail; three days of anguish Emilio thought would never end. He didn't tell anybody in school.

"Why are you so quiet lately? Ever since Kathy's birthday you seem different. I thought you had a good time, learning to skate and all," said Ali at lunch, two days after the party. The boys were in line waiting to get their lunch.

"There's nothing wrong. Why do you say that?"

"You've been kind of weird," said Ali.

Matt suddenly appeared in front of them, interrupting their conversation. "These worms are having lunch. Why aren't you eating dirt? You stinky kids made me and Cato believe Ali was hurt. Like we care. He isn't hurt. Look at him! Wait 'til we *really* hurt you." He laughed and walked away.

Emilio and Ali had kept the bullies away by making them believe Ali was waiting for the results of a medical test. They had told them Ali had a bump inside his head and might have to have surgery.

"Ignore them," said Ali, looking for a place to sit.

"I'm not afraid of them anymore, at least not as much as before. Do you think they can really hurt us?" asked Emilio.

"I thought you said you weren't afraid. Sooner or later they'll get tired of bothering us. If they know we are afraid, they'll never stop," said Ali.

"I know that. I also know they'll respect us, and soon. You'll see," said Emilio, putting his tray on the table.

"Let's forget Matt and tell me why are you acting weird." Ali bit on the sandwich his mother prepared for him every day. He took his lunch to school and bought only milk and dessert from the school cafeteria.

Emilio didn't want to tell Ali about his brother. "I had a fight with my brother and my mother is mad at me." He was not quite lying. When Jaime had come home he was so upset they had the worst fight ever. His mother was angry at both of them. Emilio looked at the mushy food in front of him. It was disgusting.

"I don't have any brothers or sisters, no one to fight with. It's only my mother and me." Ali seemed subdued.

"Where is your father?" asked Emilio.

"I don't know. Mama said he left us when I was a baby and never heard from him again. I wish I could have known him." Ali's eyes looked sad. "Mama's brother helped us come to this country. A neighbor from New York moved to Houston and got Mama a job here."

"I don't have a father either." Emilio paused. He didn't want to talk about his father, not after what Jaime had done. Emilio had not talked to his father in several days because he felt that his father's spirit was troubled by what had happened. "I'm through eating. I have to go study math."

"Why math? We don't have a test or anything," said Ali.

"I can't tell you yet. You'll find out if I can pull it off." Emilio stood up, ready to go.

"You're acting really weird lately, Emilio. I don't like it. We're friends. Why don't you tell me?" asked Ali.

"It's bad luck to tell. Besides, I don't know if I can do it. See you later." Emilio walked away before his friend could say anything else.

Emilio was sorry he had told Ali about studying math. He had meant to keep the project to himself and was determined to succeed. It was the only way for him to show his family, friends, and enemies that he was as good as any one else.

The teacher had let the class know about the math contest, but no one seemed to have paid attention. At first he didn't consider the possibility. It came to him suddenly: He knew his father wanted him to do it. From that moment on Emilio decided to do everything he could to win.

Emilio liked to learn and believed he was good with numbers. During the next couple of months he had to become the best if he wanted to compete.

"Do you want to go with Marcia, Pablo, and me

to a movie Saturday?" asked Clara after school.

"I can't this Saturday. I'm sorry, Clara. See you later," said Emilio, walking away. It was going to be difficult to explain to his friends why he couldn't do things with them for the next few weeks.

"Wait, Emilio, let's walk together. I want to talk to you!" yelled Clara.

Emilio heard her but played deaf. He had to hurry to the library. He only had a couple of hours before dinner.

It wasn't easy to study at home. His mother was always sending him on errands, and Victoria wanted him to play with her. Now that Jaime was coming home early from school, he had made it his business to make Emilio pay for telling their mother about the *pandilla*. Herminia had promised the police that she would keep Jaime home after school.

"Where have you been, Emilio?" asked Herminia. "Every day you come home later than the day before. Are you also in some kind of trouble? I don't think I could take another . . ." Herminia looked distressed.

"I was studying at the library. I want to get good grades. Why don't you believe me?" asked Emilio. "I'm not Jaime."

"I never expected Jaime to do what he did. How can I trust any of you now?"

"You can look for me there any time you want,"

said Emilio, putting his books on the kitchen table.

"Well, if it isn't San Emilio," said Jaime, sarcastically. He was watching television in the main room.

Emilio didn't answer. He wasn't in the mood for another fight. "Are we eating now, Mama?"

"In a minute. Go call Victoria. Jaime, set the table," ordered Herminia.

"Why me? Victoria is in charge of that." Jaime walked back to the main room.

"Jaime, come here. You have responsibilities in this family. I've been too lenient with you and it hasn't done you any good. Do what I say." Herminia's voice was soft, as if she were afraid of her older son, who was several inches taller than her.

Jaime mumbled something but complied with his mother's wishes. Emilio left the room to call his sister.

They ate in silence, as they had done ever since Jaime went to jail. Something bad and shameful hung over them. They didn't talk about it. Even Victoria seemed to realize something bad has happened to her family.

Before Emilio went to bed he thought of the plans he had made. Was he kidding himself, thinking he had a chance to win the contest?

"Papa, I need your help. I want to do this more than anything in the world. I don't know if I'm smart enough, but something inside me tells me this is the only way. Can you put in a good word for me? I'll appreciate it. *Buenas noches*," he said before he closed his eyes to go to sleep.

The Test

"What's happening to you?" asked Clara, catching up with Emilio after Science class. "Why are you avoiding me and everyone else? Have we done something to you?"

"No, of course not. You know I like you—*very much.*" Emilio had no intention of putting his feelings into words, even though he had wanted to tell Clara for a long time how much she meant to him, but couldn't bring himself to do it.

Clara seemed surprised at first, but then her face turned red. She dropped a book, rushing to pick it up before Emilio had time to react. They were silent for what seemed an eternity to Emilio.

"Then why are you behaving like you don't want to have anything to do with anybody?" asked Clara, regaining her composure.

"It isn't you, or the others, really. I can't tell you now. I want it to be a surprise. I don't know if it'll work," said Emilio, not wanting to look Clara in the eyes.

"Why the mystery? When will you be back to yourself again?" Clara walked slightly ahead of Emilio.

Emilio didn't answer.

"Let me know when we can be friends again. I'm late for my next class."

"Yeah, me too. I'll see you. I'm your friend, even if I'm acting weird," said Emilio as they parted.

"You think you're so cool now that you learned to speak English," said José at recess. "Don't you remember how many times I had to translate for you? Now you barely talk to me."

"Since when do you want me to talk to you and be your friend?" Emilio looked at José distrustfully. "You've always been mean to me, so don't expect me to talk to you."

"I just . . . well . . . It was Matt's and Cato's idea to bother you."

What was José planning? Emilio didn't think the boy in front of him had turned into Mr. Nice from one moment to the next. "What's on your mind?"

"Nothing. I thought we could . . . be kind of friends," said Jose, looking down.

"Why now? Did you have a fight with Matt and Cato?" Emilio did not trust José at all now. "Did they put you up to something? I don't believe you want to be my friend."

"I don't like to go around with them anymore. They're—well, let's don't talk about them. I know I was mean to you and I'm sorry." José looked contrite.

Emilio was sure José was up to something. "I'll see you later. I'm going to the library."

Emilio walked away without waiting for a response.

During the next few weeks Emilio barely talked to his friends or family. They almost forgot him, looking at him as if he were an abstract figure, entering classrooms and home without being actually present.

Clara and Ali seemed mad at him. *Let them be*, he thought. *They don't understand.*

"God, I hope all of this is worth it," Emilio prayed in a low voice, one night before he went to sleep. He hadn't planned to hurt his friends. But he couldn't tell anyone. He couldn't face defeat if they knew.

The next day was the day he feared, the day his life could change.

Only the math teacher and Herminia knew about his project. He had been forced to tell his mother so that she would go easy on him with his chores. It pained him that she didn't seem confident about his performance in the competition, making Emilio even more determined to succeed.

"Hasta la tarde, Mama, I've to get going. I don't want to be late." Emilio walked around the kitchen as if looking for something.

"You have to eat breakfast first," said Herminia, rubbing her eyes. She was still in her nightclothes. "Where are you going so early? It's not even seven yet."

"Today is the math competition, Mama. Did your forget it? You never pay attention to me. If I win I can go to Washington and compete there."

"Is it today? I can't keep up with everything. There is so much to do." Herminia was talking more to herself than to her son.

"If it were Jaime you'd remember." Emilio's bitterness surfaced unexpectedly, surprising him.

"That's not true, Emilio. Don't make things more difficult. You're a good boy and I don't need to worry about you so much, at least not yet. Stop walking around and eat your cereal."

"I can't eat. I'm too nervous. Besides, you know I don't like cereal." Emilio didn't think he could swallow a sip of water.

"Here, at least eat a couple of tortillas." Herminia took a lump of dough out of the refrigerator, grabbed an old skillet from a cabinet, spread a little oil, made a tortilla with her hands and began to cook.

"Don't do that, Mama, I don't have time."

"You can't think if you don't eat. Don't argue with me." Herminia went on cooking and making tortillas. "Call Jaime and Victoria while the tortillas are still hot."

Emilio obeyed without saying anything. It was easier than arguing with his mother. He was feeling bad for making her feel guilty. His mama loved him. He knew that.

"They were very good. Bye, Mama."

"Buena suerte, hijo. Que el Espíritu Santo te ilumine," said Herminia.

"Gracias." Emilio grabbed the last tortilla and ran out the door. His mother was right; he had to eat, so he forced the food down his throat as he walked to the bus stop.

Emilio's legs felt like cotton as he entered the room where the competition would take place. He had given himself plenty of time since he didn't know the area well. His teacher had drawn a map for him but he still had to ask directions at a florist's shop when he got off the bus. At the school there were lots of arrows pointing to the room he had just entered.

There were a few students already scattered around the place. Emilio went to the back and sat down to wait for instructions. The palms of his hands were wet, and his mouth was dry.

"Good morning," said a stern-looking woman as she walked into the room a few minutes later.

"Good morning," echoed dozens of students.

"The first part of the competition will be a written test, and the second will be oral. You have two hours to finish the written test," said the woman.

A thin young man handed out the tests. Emilio glanced at his. He couldn't read it. The letters danced all over the page as if they were teasing him.

"Oh, God! What's happening to me?" Emilio closed his eyes for a moment and opened them again. The letters had gone back to form words and sentences Emilio read slowly.

"You may begin *now*," ordered the stern woman.

As he went on writing and answering questions he became calmer, regaining the confidence he thought had vanished. Emilio finished half an hour before the deadline was up, enough time for him to go over every question.

After a short break—which he used to get a drink, go to the bathroom, and splash cold water on his face—he was back in his seat. He needed all the coolness he could get to go through the oral exam.

"Danny Lawson, come to the front. Write the following equation on the board."

He heard the voice as if it had come from another world. There was a panel of two men and two women, shooting questions to a short, chubby boy who was scribbling numbers on the board.

One by one, boys and girls went to the front to answer whatever the panel asked. Two girls and one boy had run out of the room, crying. Others had turned mute, as if what they knew had been erased from their minds. Many had answered and written down results Emilio couldn't make out.

"Emilio Orduz."

It took him a moment to realized his name had been called. Without feeling the floor under his feet, Emilio walked to the front. He heard somebody talking to him but couldn't understand what he had said.

"Would you repeat the question, please?" Emilio was ready to run out, as fast and as far as he could.

Emilio, you know you can do it. You have studied and prepared yourself for this. Go on, do it. It was his father's voice, as clear as he had ever heard it. *I'm proud of you, son.*

From then on Emilio answered every question and wrote numbers and equations, solving problem after problem. There was nothing he couldn't do.

"Congratulations, you were *great,*" said a tall girl as they left the room. "I've seen you in school. I'm in the class a year ahead of you."

"Thank you, I'm sorry, I don't remember seeing you. Are there any more kids from our school?"

"Two more. I saw their names on the list. I hope you win. Bye now." The girl smiled and left.

As he walked to the bus stop the word *win* went around and around inside his head. *Win?* Me, *win?* Emilio was afraid even to consider it. I won't think about it. But he knew the wait would be extremely difficult. "Thank you Papa. I hope I—" Emilio didn't finish putting the thought into words. His bus had arrived to take him back home.

A Day of Suspense

"Do you really want to go with us to the movies?" asked Ali the next day after school. "I thought you didn't have time for your friends any more."

"Yes, I want to go with you," Emilio said meekly, caressing the book where he had hidden the piece of paper that was making him feel wild. "I'm through with what I was doing."

"So you want to go with us tonight because you don't have anything better to do? Well, how *lucky* can we get?" said Clara.

"That's not fair. I was . . . I can't tell you now, but it has nothing to do with not wanting to be friends with all of you." Emilio thought hard for something nice to say. He knew he was not good at these things. At that moment it was difficult for him to think of anything else but the invitation hidden inside his math book.

"Well, okay, let's leave it alone. But, we still aren't happy with your attitude," said Ali, who, along with Clara, had made it clear to Emilio they were upset with his strange behavior during the last several weeks.

"You'll understand soon. It's Friday. Where are we going? I love Fridays." He smiled broadly. It felt good to be hanging around the kids who had made life in his new country so much nicer.

"We aren't sure," said Marcia, joining the trio. She seemed to have become less serious than when Emilio first met her.

"I wish we could go to one of the new shows instead of always having to go to the dollar movies," said Ali.

"Sooner or later we get to see all of them. I'm glad I can go. In Conchagua, I didn't see *any* movies." For the first time Emilio realized he had found something he liked better than back home.

"Let's meet at the entrance before five," said Clara. "I've got to get going. Mama wants me to help her with the cooking tonight. I'll ask Kathy to go with us. We haven't seen her in a while."

"Okay, see you later," said Emilio, leaving the group.

He was thrilled and anxious, yet afraid to think about the letter he had received. Earlier, his math teacher had handed him an invitation to the awards ceremony. *What if? No. They probably invited all the others. Did they?* His mind went on and on, speculating, dreaming, hoping. "I don't want to think about it. I won't," mumbled Emilio.

That evening as the three of them walked back home after the movies, Emilio said, "Clara, Ali, you're my best friends. I want you to go with me, a week from Saturday, to an awards ceremony.

Would you go?"

"Awards ceremony?" asked Ali. "What are you talking about?"

"You'll find out then. Don't expect anything special. I just thought it'll be fun to go."

"Why did they invite you?" asked Clara, looking surprised.

"It's a long story. I'll tell it to you later," said Emilio.

"I'm tired of your hush-hush stuff," said Ali in an irritated voice. "Why don't you just tell us what you're up to?"

"Put up with me for a little longer, please. I promise I'll tell you all about it after the ceremony."

"You only want the two of us to go?" asked Clara.

"Yes, that's why I waited for Pablo, Marcia, and Kathy to leave. You know I like them, but I only want the two of you to come with me. Besides, I can only invite a few people. Don't ask any more questions, *por favor.*" Emilio became nervous. "I'll see you at school Monday. Bye!"

Emilio didn't wait for his friends to say anything. He walked away leaving them to believe whatever they wanted. He was too excited to stand still. Should he ask his mother to go? Would she feel embarrassed if he didn't win? Jaime would never let him forget it. Emilio hated making decisions. It was going to be a long week.

"Mama, remember, I'm not getting any awards tonight. It's just a nice ceremony. Don't expect anything at all." Emilio was so nervous he could hardly talk.

"Stop telling me that. It's okay if you don't get an award. You can always try next year. I'm proud of you anyway." Herminia straightened Emilio's old blue jacket she had cleaned and pressed the night before.

"You look nice, Mama. Is that a new dress?" It surprised Emilio to see his mother dressed so elegantly.

Herminia smiled at her own image in the bathroom mirror. She seemed pleased with what she saw. A pink satin dress and white high-heeled shoes transformed her short body. "*La comadre* Carmen lent this dress to me. You have to give people a good impression when you go to fancy places." She touched up her hair, which she had arranged in an elaborate style.

"It's not a fancy place. It's just an auditorium in the high school."

"Let's hurry, we don't want to be late. Victoria, are you ready?" yelled Herminia, pushing Emilio out of the bathroom.

"Do I look pretty?" asked Victoria, turning around in front of her mother and brother so they could admire her blue dress.

"*Estás muy linda*," said Herminia, grabbing

Victoria's hand. "I hope no one speaks to me in English. I asked Jaime to meet us there. I hope he goes."

Emilio didn't comment. It was like a mother to say a bunch of unrelated sentences at once. He wasn't even sure he wanted his brother there. Jaime had turned into a stranger since Emilio had told on him. They barely talked any more.

The Orduz family arrived at the high-school auditorium with enough time for Emilio to save places for Clara and Ali. He felt important just walking inside the high school, as if he already belonged there. In another year he would be a regular student in the huge school. The idea thrilled him but also frightened him. He was sure to encounter other kids like Matt even in high school.

Emilio's family sat quiet and subdued in the middle of the auditorium. The place looked festive and elegant to Emilio. He wasn't used to being in places like this. He felt special, participating in such a gathering.

"Hola," said Clara in a low voice, "May I sit here?"

"Of course," said Emilio, turning red. He looked at his mother, sitting to his left. "Mama, this is Clara, a friend from school."

"Mucho gusto, Clara." Herminia looked at the girl from head to toe.

Within fifteen minutes the place was full of

people. Emilio became agitated. What was he doing there? He had built himself up in his own eyes and in the eyes of the people he loved. He should have come alone.

"Stop wiggling like that," said Herminia, holding Emilio's arm. "You're making me dizzy."

Clara giggled and turned to talk to Ali, who sat to her right. Herminia seemed to make the girl uncomfortable.

"Ladies and gentlemen."

The voice startled Emilio. He forgot everything and everybody, focusing on what was happening on the stage.

"We are here to give special awards to those students who, through extra efforts in their own chosen field of study, have excelled in voluntary competition outside the classroom. The winners of the state competition will compete in Washington for the national award in each category. These awards will represent future college scholarships to these students." The tall, distinguished man paused, giving the audience time to applaud.

Two other important people—or so they looked to Emilio—said things he hardly understood. He was too nervous to concentrate on what they were saying. Something about the importance of education and other things that adults, especially teachers, were always preaching.

The distinguished-looking man was talking

again. He was calling the names of the contest winners. A biology award went to a chubby girl and a history award to a blond, thin boy with thick glasses. With each announcement, Emilio's heart pounded more fiercely.

"The award for mathematics is given to–Larry Bonne."

Emilio's eyes filled with tears. Why did they invite him when he didn't win? He thought he had done so well. In the back of his mind, he had expected to win. His first impulse was to get up and leave. But, he couldn't do that. Resigned, he prepared himself to endure the ceremony until the end.

"And the Junior High Mathematics award goes to Emilio Orduz."

"Emilio! Emilio! They're calling your name," yelled Clara.

"¿Qué dijeron?" asked Herminia as she heard her son's name, inquiring about what the man had said about Emilio.

"Mama, Emilio won! He won!" screamed Victoria.

Emilio looked at Clara and then turned to his mother, feeling as confused as he had ever been. He hadn't heard his name. He had closed his mind to the voice from the stage after the first math award. He didn't realize the previous award belonged to a high-school student.

"Why are you all screaming?" he asked.

"You won, didn't you hear?" asked Clara, pushing him out of his chair toward the stage.

Emilio was sure the floor had turned into cotton. He didn't feel the hard surface beneath his feet. Instinct guided him as he climbed the few steps to where the distinguished man was waiting for him.

"Congratulations, and good luck to you in Washington," said the man, giving Emilio a certificate.

Was he dreaming? Yes, of course he was. He couldn't be going to Washington, no, not him, not poor, stupid Emilio.

"Hijo, qué contenta estoy," said Herminia, embracing Emilio as she erupted in a string of Spanish sentences.

"Congratulations, Emilio. I'm so proud of you. Why didn't you tell us?" asked Clara, then hugged him as she whispered, "I like you a lot *too*."

"Good job, *amigo,"* said Ali, shaking his hand.

Emilio couldn't keep his eyes away from Clara. He felt such happiness he was afraid the moment would vanish if he closed his eyes.

A long half-hour passed by before Emilio, his family, and friends finally reached the street.

"Felicitaciones, hermano," said Jaime, appearing in front of Emilio as he came out of the auditorium.

"Where were you? I didn't see you," said Emilio.

"I sat in the back. I was curious about the mystery here. I didn't know what to expect. I'm happy for you," said Jaime, looking at his brother with a combination of pride and envy.

"Thank you." Emilio knew that something had deeply touched his older brother.

"Emilio, congratulations, I never thought you—anyway, you did it," said José, extending his hand.

Emilio could tell José was envious and jealous, but he also detected respect in his voice.

"Why are you here?" asked Emilio, surprised to see him.

"Someone I know saw you when you took the test, so I decided to come," said José.

So that was why Jose wanted to be my friend the other day, thought Emilio, remembering how nice he had been to him.

"Come with me over to the other side of the building, please?" asked José.

"Why?" asked Emilio. "You can talk to me here." He didn't trust the curly-haired boy.

"Someone wants to talk to you. Don't worry, nobody is going to hurt you."

"We'll be watching," said Ali, following Emilio and José.

"I'll be right back," called Emilio to his brother, who didn't know what was going on.

"Hi," said Matt, looking at Emilio in a strange way. "I just wanted to tell you we should have a truce, agreed?"

"Why now?" asked Emilio.

"Because I *say* so, agreed?" he asked again.

"Agreed," said Emilio, shaking hands with his former enemy. "There is one condition. I never want to hear you calling me stupid again."

"Okay, Emilio," said Matt, looking away for a moment. "See you."

"Yeah, see you."

"I made it, Papa, at least for now," Emilio said quietly. "I hope you're proud of me. I couldn't have done it without your help. *Gracias*."

"Emilio, Mama said we're going to celebrate in a restaurant, with your friends and all. Isn't it grand?" yelled Victoria.

"Yes, Victoria, everything is grand."